NICK ALANZO

UNDERCOVER

By

Patricia A. Florio

NICK ALANZO: UNDERCOVER

Copyright © 2025 Patricia A. Florio

Publisher Information

America Publishers
Email:info@americapublishers.com
Phone: +1 (617) 334-5774

ISBN Information

eBook: 978-1-966198-63-5
Paperback: 978-1-966198-64-2
Hardcover: 978-1-966198-65-9

Cover Design by: America Publishers

Printed in the United States of America

1st Edition: February, 2025

DEDICATION

La Famiglia

This book is dedicated to the people in my family who worked in law enforcement. My brother-in-law Frank was a mounted police officer in Coney Island and Prospect Park. Frank shined his gold buttons every night with a polishing machine. Like most of the men in blue of the New York City Police Department, he was proud of his uniform.

My husband's uncle, Salvatore Baratto, was a sergeant in the New York City Police Department's 60th Precinct on Lawrence Avenue in Brooklyn.

My brother-in-law Dominic (Nick Alanzo) is my husband's stepbrother. Nick was designated a hero, shot in the line of duty, and honored with the title Gold Star Detective by the New York City Police Department.

Jerry Baratto, another of Ralph's uncles, a Riker's Island prison guard, and served the City of New York for over forty years.

Jude R. Florio, New York City Police Department, Bushwick, Brooklyn, 82nd Precinct from 1991 until 2011.

On the Fire Fighters' side of the family: Lieutenant Anthony (Sonny) Cataldo and Robert Ward in action on 9/11. We will never forget.

I'm also dedicating this book to my grandparents, all four of them, who left their homes in Italy to come to the United States. Because of their bravery and determination, I am a product of their belief in democracy and the American way. Because of them, I have a family who settled in Brooklyn, in an Italian Ghetto, and my paternal grandparents who settled on Mott Street in Lower Manhattan. It probably wasn't easy for them to be on board a ship that had hundreds of sick people that they were travelling alongside.

They were all looking for adventure. They had no other choice. If they stayed in Italy, they would have eventually died of starvation. Instead, they were brave and relocated to a new country that had opportunities.

My father's parents, Giuseppe and Amolia believed the streets of America were lined with gold. I guess they were shocked when they arrived and saw the sidewalks were made of concrete. I know several things about both sets of grandparents.

On the Prano side of the family, my mother's father and mother came from Palermo, Sicily on board the Perugia. I have the manifest sheet which shows Petrina and Giovanni, and their three-year-old son Salvatore who arrived in New York City at Ellis Island on May 4, 1904.

I have explained their travel and arrival in depth in my book *Cucina Amelia, My Mother's Favorite Recipes from the Sicilian and Neapolitan Tradition.*

Grandpa Giovanni was a baker by trade in Italy, and that's what he continued to do until the Great Depression of 1939.

Oddly enough, the Prato side of my family (Prato and Prano), my mother changed one letter in her last name when she married my father. His family came from Avelino, Italy.

They lived in the village of Prato La Sera. I have visited this town to trace my ancestry, and I found the church of San Pelligrino. It was the church my grandparents went to.

They too set sail for America in the early 1900s. I don't have as much information about them as I do about my Sicilian ancestors. And it's sad that I have yet to visit the town they came from. I've been to Sicily on board a cruise ship and Palermo was not one of the cities we visited. But it is certainly next on my list.

To all my cousins on both sides of my family, you are in my heart and soul. I find it amazing that both sides of my family had nine children. My material grandparents had four sons and five daughters. My paternal grandparents had three daughters and six sons. But this story doesn't start with them – not because it isn't important – but this story starts on February 22, 1973.

TABLE OF CONTENT

CHAPTER ONE

FEBRUARY 1973

You might be asking yourself, why, the author, is jumping forward some seventy-odd years to tell us this story. I truly don't know why I chose to start where I am beginning, except for the fact that one of my own children was born on this day. Washington's Birthday 1973.

It was nine in the morning, and I was admitted to Community Hospital in the Flatbush section of Brooklyn. My OBGYN, Doctor Leonard Schnipper, had three pregnant women come into the hospital that morning at the same time. He planned on inducing all of us to give birth sometime that day. But the joke was on Doctor Schnipper because my child refused to come into the world.

Three nurses tried to catch this bald fast-paced doctor as he went from operating room to operating room. He was a Jewish doctor and did things ass backways. That's how my sister Molly speaks: she's always saying ass ways forward, or ass ways backward. I can't tell you what that means. But from first her name, you can tell she was named for Grandma Amolia. Molly was fourteen and a half years older than me. My brother Joe was ten years older than me. I guess I was in the accident. But this kid I was giving birth to was no accident. He was planned and we were ready to greet him or her.

In our family, we were all named after someone. That's how Italians get their names. But I had a different idea about this child I had been carrying for nine months. I was going to break the mold. My child, if a boy, would be named Jude Jason. My husband didn't like the name Ralph. We realized we would be insulted Ralph's father Big Ralph, but we were young and foolish and didn't care. If it was a girl, we named her Kristin, after Jesus, our way of saying thank you to the higher powers in our lives. We would give – if it was a girl – the middle name of Mary, honoring my husband's mother and the Blessed Mother at the same time.

One thing I could tell you about that morning of February 22, 1973, I was woman on the gurney yelling, "Get this baby out of my belly!" I had had it with labor pains. I had been in labor since January 31. I'm not kidding. I was admitted into the hospital on the evening of January 31. 1973. My due date was

February 4th. I was a few days early. They prepared and got me ready to deliver my baby.

Three hours later, on that cold night at the end of January, the hospital sent me home. The doctors and nurses agreed, I wasn't ready yet, only to be told to check in with the doctor at his office the next morning.

I was frustrated. I had delivered twins six years earlier with no problem. What was the hold-up?

"Jesus, help me." How could I not cry out for Jesus? I was dying in pain and I really believed nobody cared. "What, no baby, yet. This is bullshit!"

I find I have a dirty mouth when things aren't going my way. With a few other choice words, I left the hospital and went home.

My husband knew he was in for it. I couldn't wait to get him home alone. I was going to give him a piece of my mind.

Then on the morning on February 22, 1973, he took me back to Community Hospital in the Flatbush section of Brooklyn, where I waited for a Dr. Schnipper to administer ^ Pitocin, a drug that induces labor pains.

I was a sweaty mess, and I also realized how much I hated Dr. Schnipper, my husband, and all the men in the free world. I hated the nurses, too. I hated everyone. The only belief I held onto was that God would come and rescue me.

At some point they must have knocked me out, because I don't remember anything after they inserted the needle in my back.

From somewhere in the back of the operating room, I heard Dr. Schnipper's snappy voice saying, "Pat, you have fine healthy another son."

Oh, fuck, I thought, one more son. Now I have three. Who's going to help me take care of these kids. Certainly, not my mother. She hated me for marrying Ralph. My father was deceased. He had passed away several years earlier when the twins were a year old.

My poor father. He hated me too. That's a long story, one day, I'll tell you why. He was sitting in his favorite chair reading a detective paperback, probably Mickey Splaine. We found him with the book in his lap. He had had a fatal heart attack in the summer of 1967.

My brother-in-law Frank had just rung the outside bell. He had come to borrow my father's car to take his family on our yearly cousins' picnic. Frank is a New York City Police Officer. He told me to dial 911.

I did, while Frank tried to resuscitate my father. The ambulance came within a matter of minutes; my grief-stricken mother was screaming at the top of her lungs from my apartment on the top floor.

We didn't have our cousins' picnic that summer. We had a wake for my father instead. My sister-in-law gave me a blue pill. Life became a blur. I had no idea what had taken. I had never taken a drug before.

Life was kind of upside down at this point. I was depressed. I stayed home a lot. Three kids, the house was a disaster. My mother called me a pig. I felt useless. All that staying in the house watching daytime TV got to me. That's when Ralph had this brilliant idea that I should become a note reader.

Note reading is a skill, just like court reporting. It's the type of job where you read court reporters' notes and type up transcripts of cases. It's like court reporting, in that you must be a good typist and practice, practice, practice, practice, like going to Carnegie Hall, or reading another language.

My mother hated living with us. She went back to Brooklyn to live. It had to be this way because she was hiding the absentee cards from Tottenville High Scheel, where Anthony and Joseph were *supposedly* going to school.

Mama didn't know the twins wanted to quit high school in their senior year. "Quit School! Bullshit," Ralph said. "You are not quitting school. You are going to get jobs, both of you, get jobs, or get the hell out of this house."

They got jobs. Anthony woke up every morning at 4 a. m. and drove out to Long Island, where he hot-walked horses. Joseph found a job as a carpenter, framing houses. They were both great with their hands. Anthony eventually got his GED and became a plumber for the City of New York and climbed in and out of sewers. The Art Carney of our family. But he never complained. He made a lot of money and bought a new home in New Jersey. He's a great decorator too. Anthony can do just about anything. Ask his girlfriend Maria. She bought a house near him and is a wonderful cook and companion.

Joseph manages a car dealership; why we drive Toyotas. He always said, "Once a Toyota owner, you will never buy anything else."

That's true. Even though we live in Florida now, and I drive very little, we still own a Toyota Camry, the kind you don't have to fill with gas. My husband brags he can get 60 miles with a tank of gas. I'm going to try to drive. I like Carolas: they are only $300 a month to lease.

That's not the end of this story. I have so much more to tell all of you!

You know my granddaughter, Amelia Hope. She's the love of my life. So is her mother, Kristin. I gave Amelia, who is named after my mother, the middle name of Hope. I did that because she's the hope of my life.

It's time I told you about Nick Alanzo. After all, he is the hero of this book. He decided after finishing up at Erasmus High School, that he would go to Brooklyn College and get 60 credits to join the police department's academy and become a man in blue.

Nick or Dominic was my mother-in-law Mary's stepson. He had tough teenage years. He had gotten involved with the wrong people. Drug dealers, and potheads.

Not much substance. He felt sorry for his older brother. And thought of him as a loser. Like whom would love a guy like Ralph. A pathetic bowler, who practiced a hundred games a week in the bowling alley where I so happened to work after I was divorced, that's where I happened to get a job. I knew the owners and they asked me to manage the bowling alley. They introduced me to Ralph as a professional bowler who would come and practice his games, and he would also provide instruction to anyone interested in learning a few things about holding the ball: three or four-step approach. I liked

Ralph. He was a nice person. His brother Nick was a big-mouth idiot.

One morning, Ralph came over to the front desk where I rented shoes, and said, "Let's play chess for your body."

"What do I win?" I asked.

"Oh, cute, very cute," he quipped.

I played him for his body, and he lost. But it wasn't his body I wanted. It was his conversation. I was a good chess player in those days, but I really had no men friends to talk. I had been dating, but it wasn't going very well.

I had beat him at his game of chess. According to lore, I had beaten the best. But I didn't want his body. I wanted him to come home with me and meet my mother. I knew my mother wouldn't be ready for me to be with another man since my divorce, but I did have an annulment, so I could get married in the Catholic church one day.

My friend Father Richie told me about his uncle, who happened to be the Bishop of Brooklyn. He had the Tribunal for the Catholic Church in the Bishop's House on Green Avenue in the Greenpoint section of Brooklyn. That's where we picked up Thomas every morning. Now, I'm getting ahead of myself. I do that a lot. I'll slow down.

While Ralph was going to Stenotype Institute in Manhattan, I wrote hundreds of words in a notebook about my first marriage, trying to convince the Bishop that I was too young to enter the contract of marriage. I had been in love with someone else at the time.

Yes, I will admit. I was a flighty teenager, and stayed looney into my twenties, I flirted a bit too much. I was never settled about love. What was this great burst of energy that love was supposed to make a girl or woman do crazy things. I was not particularly attractive. Now, I'm selling myself short. I certainly wasn't ugly. I did like this guy who worked around the corner from where we lived, the house my father died in. Vincent was crazy about me. Those are his exact words. But I wasn't crazy about him. I was in love with Ralph. I wanted to marry him Ralph somewhere deep inside. I just knew he was a good person.

Ralph was my bowling instructor, and he loved my sons. We were going to run away to Las Vegas and get married on the Professional Bowlers tour.

I was 28 years old. What could my mother say? Anthony and Joseph were six years old. They were okay staying out at my brother's home in Port Jefferson while I went on my very first trip along. They wanted a father, and they loved Ralph. They wanted Ralph to be their father. We all loved him. I don't know why I had to wait for my father to die. I was such a frightened kid. I feared my father. It could be because he flew off the handle. Old Italian mentality about having a daughter.

I had come home late one night, just by ten minutes. I was already working a full-time job on Broad Street in Manhattan. My father met me halfway from the bus stop, that I had just walked from, dragged me home and beat the living crap out of me. Why? I have no idea. Frustration, I guess.

When daddy said nine o'clock, he meant 9 o'clock and not ten minutes after nine.

Here I am having had my third child. And I was on a train going to Manhattan because of my husband. He generally got up at 6 a. m. and went into the bowling alley where he was now the manager and opened the place. When he lit the grill, someone had already turned the pilot off, so the match ignited the gas line, BOOM! Flames came flying out from everywhere.

I called the bowling alley that morning to wish my husband a good morning, and to wish him luck at the tournament. I had no idea that he had burned the hair off his arms and head.

The snack bar worker who picked up the phone blurted out, "Don't worry, Pat, Ralph is okay. He only singed his hair off his arms. And a little hair from his head. Pat, listen, while I'm telling you this. I think you should know that a detective came into the bowling alley this morning to see Ralph. His stepbrother Nick had been shot making a narcotics buy. Ralph didn't want me to tell you. He was afraid you'd get upset. So please don't rat me out. I thought you should know."

Hearing this, I panicked and dropped the phone. I yelled downstairs to my mother. "Mom, you have to watch the baby. Ralph got hurt this morning. I'm going to New York City. I didn't say anything to her about Nick. I just wanted to get out of the house as fast as I could. Why tell an old woman that someone had been shot. I didn't know the nature of his wounds and I didn't want her to worry. My in-laws were on their first vacation in Las Vegas, and I didn't want my mother jumping the gun and calling them.

This was not going to be a good day. As I prepared myself for the unknown, I started to chart my path.

The F train was right around the corner from our house. I ripped off my pajamas and took a quick shower. I jogged the block and a half to the train station on Eighteenth Avenue and McDonald and I waited on the platform freezing. I hadn't dressed properly, and a chill ran through my body. My lips quivered, probably from the cold and the fear gripping my heart.

I sat next to the window and looked at the cloudy sky. Rain was in the air. I hadn't taken an umbrella, but what did it matter. I was in a panic. My husband, my brother-in-law, they both needed me, and I ran, ran, ran.

A million thoughts went racing in my mind; what would I say? What would I do when I got into Madison

Square Garden? I prayed. I believed in Mary our Blessed Mother. I pulled out a pair of rosary beads that someone had given to me from Rome. I began by holding the cross and whispering "I believe in God, the Father Almighty, creator of heaven and earth..."

I began to feel a little better. When I was a high school student I went to mass every morning. While the train was rocking me, I thought about the day Sister Mary Peter called me over to the convent, and said, "Pat, I believe you have a calling from Jesus."

I was stunned. You could have knocked me over with a feather duster. A calling from God. I said nothing. I just stood there waiting for her next phrase. "I think you should go away with Jane and Denise; they are going on a vocational retreat. I believe you should seek it out."

Why was I thinking about all this now? That happened years ago when I was just seventeen years old. I'd give anything to go back to those days when homework was my only problem. Now I had a husband who had burned himself. I had a brother-in-law who had been shot. What was God trying to tell me?

Back in those high school days, I was a simple child, so I followed Sister Mary Peter's advice, and I went to Mount Kissko to a vocational retreat at the order of the Canticle Sisters. A cloistered order of nuns who woke every morning at four a. m. to chant and say the rosary. It was a beautiful experience. I wasn't sorry I was there to experience how they lived.

They prayed for the world. I couldn't think of praying for the world at that minute, but I did pray for my husband and for Nick.

At the 50th Street Station, I ran up the flight of stairs from the subway and two blocks over to Madison Square Garden. I rode the escalator up to the bowling lanes, and I found my husband's name on the chart, and I stood behind him as he was about to throw his eleventh strike. One more and he would have bowled a perfect game. At least I knew he was all right. What about Nick? Would Nick be alright? If he was dead, Ralph wouldn't have been bowling. That thought comforted me.

I kept saying over and over in my head: Nick was all right. Nick was all right. Nick was all right. It was my mantra for that time and place. I think I have psychological problems; I whispered to myself.

I didn't allow Ralph to see me, as he had one more strike to throw. Shit! A hanging ten pin! Go figure, he threw a 299. A lot of back slaps and hand slaps from his fellow bowlers. I wanted to throw my arms around him and take him to the hospital where Nick was being treated, but I didn't want to ruin his day. He was smiling. He was happy. Who was I to take him away from all this celebration? But I knew we had to call Mary and Big Ralph in Las Vegas.

I know Mary. She wasn't a strong person like me. She would fold. Nick was her first child out of wedlock. She was being punished for her sins. Why was she still being punished? Nick meant a lot to her. He saved her life. I understood Mary.

When I wanted to break off my engagement with another man, my father said, "No, all brides have cold feet." My father made me get married to someone I didn't love. Then Ralph came into my life.

I wish my father lived to know my husband. I know in my heart they would have been good friends. My mother finally came around and then she started calling Ralph her boyfriend.

I thought about my mother. Hey, Ma, I know you're home taking care of my baby, but why did you have to give me such a hard time? I was a woman, twenty-eight years old. Sometimes I did know what I was doing. Maybe I wasn't as smart as you. But look at me, Mom, I'm married, and I have three sons, and Ralph has adopted my twins. I'm a lucky woman. Aren't I?

She's never going to give me the satisfaction of saying I'm a good mother. But that's okay because I know I'm a good mother and that's all that counts.

Ralph finally spots me in the crowd.

"What are you doing here?"

"I left Jude with my mother. I heard about Nick. And you burned your arm and the front of your hair. Oh, shit, Ralph, you have no eyebrows. "

"I know he says," and just laughs. Those two chipped teeth make him adorable in my eyes.

"We can leave around noontime, and we'll go and check on Nick. I spoke to his captain. He's going to be all right. He may never shoot a gun again, but he's going to be all right. "

"Do you think he will have to quit the police department?

"I don't know," Ralph said with a pained look on his face.

CHAPTER TWO

DOMINIC (NICK) ALANZO

Dominic tortured my in-laws while Ralph was away in Vietnam. It was the sixties. Summer of Love. Timothy O'Leary. Drugs. Strawberry Fields. The Beatles. Woodstock. A combination of drugs and aggression made up Nick's teenage years.

He went to school, but knew he wasn't going to college. He didn't want to go. And he refused to go into the Army. He avoided the draft by having high blood pressure.

He'd rather hang out with his friends. If you could call them friends.

One night, while my mother-in-law watched television from her Brooklyn apartment where big Ralph was the superintendent. There was a knock on the door. When Mary answered the door, someone had dropped off Nick, totally naked, and convulsing from LSD. This was not the first time he had fooled with drugs like this, and cocaine, and other types of hallucinogens.

Mary and her husband put him in his room. Mary called her brother who was a sergeant in the 60th Precinct in Brooklyn. Sal came to the house, and he took care of Nick throughout the night. It was a mess. Nick was a big fat kid. He weighed over 200 pounds as a teenager. He hated himself and started to take diet pills. This created a need for more drugs, until he was hooked.

Sal took care of Nick for the next two days. They took him to a psychologist, a friend of Sal's from the police department. This guy had a great effect on Nick, so much so that Nick started to believe he could turn his life around.

When Ralph, Jr. came back from Vietnam and saw Nick for the first time, he didn't know who he was. Nick had lost over seventy-five pounds, was as thin as a rail, and had long dirty black hair and a beard.

Mary said to Ralph, "That's your brother Nick. I know you don't recognize him. He's doing great. He completed sixty credits at Brooklyn College and he's going to go to the Police Academy."

Nick had always been a complicated kid. Cutting school, running around with the wrong crowd. He was finally going to settle down and get married. Nick never liked Ralph, Jr. He felt sorry for him, "Oh, the poor bowler. He doesn't even know how to earn a living. Who could ever love him?"

"Me, that's who, your piece of garbage. You've given your parents nothing but heartache. Ralph is a good person. No matter what you think. He's just getting home from the Army. Give him a chance. He will prove you all wrong."

It was like the days of *Wine and Roses* – if I can use that analogy. My brother-in-law Nick always had a chip on his should. He was always so nasty and righteous. I wanted them all to give Ralph a break. He had just gotten home from Vietnam and when I met him, I fell in love with him. He was my cup of tea. The cream in my coffee. Fuck you, Nick, go marry your girlfriend. Leave us alone.

It all went running through my mind like the F train chugging along the tracks up to Madison Square

Garden. I had made up my mind, I wasn't going to allow people to step all over us. We were good people. I hated to even say that about us, because it sounds so cliché. But it wasn't. We were good. We had manners. We were taught the right way. Nick took everything and he never shared what he had. That was the difference. He always felt he was entitled to something and he hurt a lot of people along the way.

CHAPTER THREE

KINGS COUNTY HOSPITAL

By the time we got there, it was about four in the afternoon. Nick had been admitted around five that morning. He had come out of surgery where they removed a bullet from his right shoulder, that had made its way into the wing of his back, and then came back out. They found the 357-magnum bullet in the elevator of the Lexon Hill Apartment. Nick was lucky that Kings County Hospital was a few blocks away from where he was shot. The doctors did a great job. The surgeon said he should retire from being a police officer. Nick didn't want to hear that.

He had made up his mind two hours after he came out of recovery that he was going back to the job. He was a narcotics agent, and he loved what he did.

The night of the shooting, Nick had been earlier that evening in Bay Ridge first. He had infra-red dye on his hands, and he patted everyone on the back that he knew who bought drugs from him.

Brooklyn South Narcotics had a great night picking up all the druggies and throwing them in the back of a patty-wagon. And Nick celebrated with his team. Then he went on to his next bust. That's when he was shot point blank.

I'm jumping around a bit, only because I want to give you a sense of how crazy Nick was.

When anyone went to visit Nick, he played the tape from the wire he wore the night he was shot.

You can hear him gasping for breath, and you can hardly make out what he was saying: "Officer down! I've been shot. I'm taking the stairway. Go to Apartment G-4, you'll find the guy who shot me in the black leather jacket, wearing black –"Then he fades out --- his team had already called an ambulance and were on their way up the flight of steps.

When Ralph and I got to the hospital, Nick was already out of surgery and was placed in bed in a private room. The curtains were pulled around his bed and there was a police officer sitting outside the door. It was like a scene from the Godfather when Don Corleone had been shot.

When Nick saw Ralph, he sat up in bed, he was bandaged in white gauze, all around his shoulder and right arm. "Ralphie, I told you hair doesn't grow on steel." And then he collapsed.

My husband broke down and cried like a baby. He sobbed for a long time. They had never been close, but this scene was too much for Ralph to bear.

Yes, Dominic Nick Alanzo, man of steel – hard head – less brains than I thought – two weeks after his stay in the hospital, he refused to retire. He wanted to go back into the Narcotics Bureau. But they insisted he stay home for about a month.

His wife would have to put up with him. We would just ignore him with his ranting and raving that he had to get back to work.

When Mary and Ralph got back from Vegas about two days later, Nick was still in the hospital. But they came back just in time to see the Mayor of New York City cite Nick as a hero, and honor him with a gold badge, the medal of honor.

Things turned out okay. Nick eventually went back to work. Desk duty at first, but shortly thereafter, he realized he couldn't do it. He had to admit it was too much for him. His mind was out of whack. He constantly played that tape of the night he was shot. He was obsessed.

My friend had a radio station in Asbury Park, *restore by the Shore,* and Nick brought the tape to her show, for all to hear in the cities that the channel picked up. Nick's story went out on the airwaves to the people of the central and southern part of New Jersey. Everyone who heard his story was impressed. He was a hero. You can't take that away from him.

Now, I'm telling his story so it will go even further. But this is not the last you will hear about Nick Alanzo, my husband's stepbrother. During his recovery, he planned to go to California and try his wit at becoming an actor.

Unfortunately, by that time, he had divorced his first wife, Ellen. Nick would get married so many times, I wouldn't be able to keep track of his wives.

He eventually made a little splash in Hollywood. He was in TV commercials with Jerry Seinfeld for American Express: *Don't leave home without it.* And he did a short clip with Roy Scheider: I believe it was *Rooftops.*

Then after a year or two, he was picked for a role in a Sergio Leone movie: *Once Upon a Time in America.*

The brothers weren't as close as they once were when they were children and lived in Newburgh, New York. Along the way, as teenagers, there were a few fallings out, especially after big Ralph died.

My father-in-law tried, as any father might, to control his stepson, but Nick didn't want any of it. He really disliked his stepfather for no other reason other than they had another son. My husband. Who is a good man, but Nick was jealous.

***

We were scheduled to meet in Italy while Nick was filming the Sergio Leone film in Germany. But we didn't know if they were talking to us. Nick had married Lola, a very nice Jewish girl. I liked her, but Nick was all over the place – secretly seeing another woman – my husband tried talking to him. But you just can't talk to the Man of Steel. He was steel chested and hardheaded.

We were walking from our apartment to the elevator in La Sicilia, our hotel on the Via Veneto. When the elevator doors opened, Lola and Nick were standing there. We hugged and kissed, and everything was forgiven.

That was a good thing. I only had eight days in Rome, and I didn't want to spend any time crying in my room. Yeah, I'm a tearjerker. I always was and I always will be. It's just my personality type. I was diagnosed by my mother's doctor when I was a child. He said I had melancholia. It's a form of depression. It would follow me all the days of my life.

In a lot of ways, I'm like Nick. He had problems when he was a child. I had depression problems too. I have never taken drugs until four years ago. After Covid, I became a recluse. I didn't go out of the house. It took me two years to see friends and talk on the phone.

At this time in my life, I'd love to talk with people who have mental health issues. I think I could help them. While I'm an author, my personal experience is valuable.

Nick came back to New York after Los Angeles, divorced Lola and married yet another woman. This time his wife became pregnant. This would be Nick's first child. They had a baby girl, and I think Nick settled down a bit. Well, for a little while anyway.

The trial was finally coming to court – and Nick would have to be a witness. He asked Ralph if he would go with him.

CHAPTER FOUR

CRIMINAL COURT BROOKLYN, NEW YORK

After the arraignment and grand jury indictment, Jeremy Ross was found guilty of shooting an officer. He had been out on bail for over a year. Then after he violated his probation, he was locked up and now he would appear for his trial. A court-appointed attorney had been assigned to him.

Now in Part 2, Judge DeSantis would hear the trial: The People of the State of New York v. Jeremy Ross.

A lot of the same police officers and detectives we had met on the day Nick was shot were still working with Brooklyn South Narcotics.

While they were in the courtroom one morning, a detective came up to my husband and asked him, "How long are you going to play Peter Pan?"

Ralph was taken aback. He was still on the professional bowlers' tour, and it wasn't going that great. He had won some regional tournaments but had not won a championship yet.

He had other jobs, like moving furniture and working laborer jobs.

"You were in Vietnam, right, Ralph?" One detective asked him.

"Yes," Ralph answered.

"Then you have the Bill of Rights. The government will pay you when you go to school. You see that guy sitting over there with the machine tucked in between his legs?"

Ralph shook his head in the affirmative.

"He's a court reporter. They make more money than the judges and lawyers combined. Why don't you investigate it. I'm telling you the Army will pay you a stipend."

My husband tells me later that he looked over at the guy in the sharkskin suit wearing a great colorful shirt and tie, and said to himself, yeah, why don't I go back to school.

When he came home and told me this, I jumped for joy. I had always wanted to go back to school myself. But my father was an old-fashioned Italian man. He didn't believe in education for girls. I busted his buns for him to send me to a Catholic high school. And I had to pay back all the tuition money when I got my first job after graduation. And since I didn't become a nun, this was my chance to see what it was like to go to college.

Ralph explored all the avenues and went back to school. In the interim, my brother Joe's brother-in-law owned a bus company transporting special needs children to school. He offered us a job. I became Ralph's morning matron. My mother Millie became Ralph's afternoon matron. In the middle of the day, Ralph went to school.

CHAPTER FIVE

OUR LONG DAYS THAT TURNED INTO NIGHTS

At six in the morning, five days a week, except for federal and Jewish holidays, I got up, showered, and left my three sons with my mother. We lived in the apartment in Brooklyn upstairs from her.

I went on the bus as Ralph's matron. First, from Brooklyn, we drove to 175th Street and Amsterdam Avenue. Then we drove through Central Park and picked up Abbie and Margaret. They were boyfriend and girlfriend, around eighteen years old but lived separately with their parents. All these children had special needs.

Ruben on 175th Street was about twenty years old. He was autistic and gave us the most problems. When I say problems, I just mean he was hard to handle. He loved running away. It was funny, but at the same time scary.

Abbie and Margaret had Down Syndrome. They loved one another, but their parents asked us if we could please keep them apart.

Bella was the cutest. She was deaf and couldn't speak. But she knew that once we crossed over onto the Brooklyn side to pick up Thomas, there was a Catholic church there, where she could see the steeple, and she'd put her fingers together and make a cross, telling us she knew we were Christian.

Then we picked up Thomas who lived in Greenpoint in Brooklyn. Our usual conversation with Thomas started with, "Ggg, ggg, goo morning, Ralph." It would take a while, but he got out his good morning greeting wishing Ralph a great day.

We dropped the kids off at Brooklyn Yeshivas where they went to school. Then Ralph drove me home, parked the bus, and took the F Train to Columbus Circle and 58th Street in Manhattan and went to class at the Stenotype Institute where he studied theory.

CHAPTER SIX

THEORY

Theory is the first thing you learn about court reporting. It's the alphabet of the machine. I don't remember what letters aren't there, but I know there are 24 keys on the machine.

The keys a reporter hits with his or her thumbs are the vowels. It's called vocalization. I know it by heart. Long E, Long O, Long A, Long I sound, using your thumbs is how you write these vowel sounds.

The first half of the machine, the left-hand side are the starting sounds. The Suffixes. On the right-hand side of the machine are the Prefixes, the ending sounds of a word. For instance, if you wanted to write the word flower. You would use your right hand to hit the F keys, then the vowels for "our" and it becomes flower.

For plural sounds, the pinky is the finger to use for the Z or S in plurals. So, I can write flowers, by using my left hand, the vowel sounds, and then the final S. It's easy. If you practice, practice, practice. That's the way you get to Carnegie Hall and that's the way you become a great court reporter.

Ralph had this great idea one morning. "You go to Stenotype on Academy Saturdays. You learn how to note read, and you can type up my transcripts."

I was eager to get out of the house. We decided to take the kids with us on the bus we were driving during the week. We paid for our own gas and Lou didn't mind us using his van for recreation. That was part of the deal.

That's when I met Mr. Piazza. He was the note reading instructor. He was also Ralph's speed class teacher. He was the gray-haired David Niven of the Academy. He was a debonaire. He walked tall like a Marine and held himself out to be a whiz. He knew something about everything. He charmed his way with the women in the class, of which there were only two. Most of the class were men. Men seemed to dominate the field of court reporting during the mid-seventies.

The only shortfall was that Ralph couldn't stay for his English classes at 2:30 in the afternoon, because he had to pick up my mother as his afternoon matron and pick up the kids from the Yeshivas and take them back home to Manhattan.

By the end of the day, Ralph would have been in Manhattan three times, and back to Brooklyn three times, have his dinner, then take the machine and sit in front of the television and practice, practice, practice.

I didn't mind working on the bus one bit. As a matter of fact, I loved being in New York City Plus, I found the Marlboro Man on one of my trips back from Manhattan. I spotted him one morning going from Manhattan into Brooklyn to pick up Thomas.

Tom Selick had a career, but he had started out advertising cigarettes, something that is not popular anymore. Lung cancer has been attributed to cigarette smoking and I remember when Ralph and I quit smoking. By this time, as we were still working on the bus, I became pregnant with my fourth child.

At least Mary and Big Ralph were ecstatic about us having another grandchild. Big Ralph kept telling me to *think pink*. Everyone wanted me to have a girl. I wanted to have a girl too.

My mother was frantic. She couldn't believe I was having my fourth child. She said she was going to move to Italy. The thought of me having another child in her house, she was thinking about the wear and tear on her. I was thinking about moving, but we couldn't move. Rents were high and we didn't have a down payment for a house.

What could I say? It happens. I guess we weren't thinking that I couldn't become pregnant again. But at least my husband was ready to graduate from Stenotype. On the morning, he was scheduled to take the civil service exam for the City of New York, I was scheduled to have a Cesarean Section to deliver my fourth child.

On the subway steps leading up to the district attorney's office in Boro Hall, Brooklyn, Ralph dropped his court reporting machine down a flight of steps. A woman who had seen this happen, offered her machine to Ralph. She had just come from the DA's office where she had taken the test.

Dr. Schnipper was ready for me this time. There would be no turning back. I was scheduled at around eleven a. m. This time I was prepared for the epidural and went right to sleep.

When I awoke, I found out I had a baby girl. Kristin was born on November 9, 1977. I finally had my daughter. She was a blessing and looked just like me. It was weird. I felt like I was looking at myself.

When Ralph found me in the recovery room, he had a big smile on his face. He had gotten the job. We finally had medical benefits, not that I was going to have any more children. But just in case. We were now covered.

CHAPTER SEVEN

MY CAREER IN COURT REPORTING

I had completed Mr. Piazza's note reading class at the Stenotype Academy in Manhattan, and I now worked from home. As my daughter played beneath my desk, I sat in my kitchen in Staten Island and typed on a Selectric typewriter. Those were the days of carbon copies. I worked several hours a day for several court reporters.

Richie Gross was one reporter that I worked for. He was a criminal court reporter. The same court Jeremy Ross was given eighteen years by Judge DeSantis for shooting my brother-in-law Nick. Richie was also doing a job for Judge DeSantis who wanted to be an author, and I remember thinking how funny the universe is: I was an author wanting to be a court reporter, and Richie was working for a judge who wanted to be an author.

Back then, I had an ambidextrous mind. I could type transcripts, throw in a load of clothes, and take care of my daughter all at the same time.

My sons were in school. It was only me and my mother, and Kristin in the house. My mother was always a pain in the ass. She checked on me several times a day, to make sure I had fed my daughter, and I wasn't neglecting cleaning while I typed on a new ball Selectric Typewriter.

I knew it was time for me to get out of the house. I was captive for eight years. While the twins were in high school, and Jude in grammar school, I thought it would be a good time for me to go back to school. Kristin was now four years old, and there were prekindergarten schools where she could go to school for half a day.

I needed air. I needed desperately to get out of the house. I felt cooped up for too many years. I started school in 1984 at the College of Staten Island.

I had heard about Marge Zemek from other reporters who had taken her course. She taught what was called back then *A Crash Course in Court Stenography.* I borrowed Ralph's old machine, and I became the woman who at six p. m. sharp every Monday night made a quick run out of the house. Ralph got to be the house-dad one day a week.

I was so excited the first night of school, I ran out without shoes on my feet. I realized it when I backed out of the driveway, and I surely wasn't going back into the house to be trapped by Kristin.

I was the woman who went to school without shoes on. Shoeless Pat stuck. It wasn't so bad. I've done crazier things in my life. Things I refuse to share in this book. I'm not a crazy woman, just a little bit insane.

I loved everything in my life. Gardening, painting, singing, dancing, going to the beach. I totally enjoyed eating and I put on quite a few pounds. I was desperate for exercise. I joined Weight Watchers and lost forty pounds. I felt better about myself.

Right around the time I was scheduled to graduate from the College of Staten Island, a job opened in the Bankruptcy Court. I was assigned to Judge Feller. My career in court reporting began.

I was not a great reporter, but I was able to make transcripts. My knowledge of the English language helped me. Then one day, I got a phone call in our offices on 75 Clinton Street in Brooklyn. One of the secretaries for one of the judges had forgotten to order a court reporter for a trial that was about to take place at the ceremonial court at 225 Cadman Plaza East.

When I got to the building, I went immediately up to the court reporters' offices. I borrowed a tape recorder from one of their reporters, and I set it up in the ceremonial courtroom.

Twenty-three attorneys showed up for a Chapter 11 confirmation hearing. That's when a company is solvent again and goes back into business. I immediately took out a piece of paper and wrote down the twelve attorneys on one side of the aisle, and the twelve attorneys on the other side of the aisle.

I swore in the witness, as Judge Holland asked me to do. The attorney for the trustee started to rapidly fire questions to the witness. I got lost somewhere between the questions and the answers. When the attorney for the trustee asked me to read back the question, I pulled up the paper from the machine and looked for the symbol I used for his name. I honestly couldn't find it. I knew it would be on the recording machine. After a few seconds, the judge asked the attorney to proceed.

"Your Honor, I just asked the reporter to read back the last question."

Judge Holland looked over at me.

I shrugged my shoulders. I could find it, or I couldn't read it. I really don't know which one. I was shaking. Oh boy, did I fuck up.

Finally, Judge Holland said, "Council, ask the question again. You're confusing my court reporter."

I could have kissed the judge. Not really! But you know what I mean. He saved me, and I'll always be eternally grateful.

When I got back to my office, I cried my eyes out. I was an idiot. When Ralph came back to the office, I told him what happened, and we sat together and made a transcript. When I received a check from the attorney for the trustee, I was grateful. I had escaped being embarrassed. I swore that would never happen again. And it never did.

CHAPTER EIGHT

THE SUMMER OF 1987

August came in like a lion. The heat was overwhelming. Going to work in the city was torture. Most judges don't work in August, or they take several days off during the week. This was a blessing and a curse. We worked on a per diem rate. Plus, a page rate. No court, no pages, no money. As simple as algebra.

Big Ralph finally had a job fit for his disposition. He liked baking cakes. At one time in his life, he was a baker at a bakery on 86th Street in Brooklyn. He always made exotic cakes for my kids. For Anthony and Joseph, he created Shay Stadium, the entire ballpark made from vanilla and chocolate cake, and blue and orange icing. The twins were thrilled. Plus, it tasted great.

For Jude, he made Mickey Mouse's face. The black ears and cherry nose. Grandpa Ralph was great. At the present time, my husband had gotten his father a job at the D. A. 's office. Elizabeth Holtman was the district attorney. She loved Ralph, Sr., and she had him run the Christmas party and all the activities and special events. My father-in-law finally had an inside job. From tarring roofs to cementing sidewalks to the dead of winter and owing a fruit and vegetable store that always went belly up, he was finally indoors. He had a pension. He had sick days. He had a job with benefits. We were all happy for him.

One morning after he took a shower to get ready for work, Mary heard something loud fall off a shelf from inside their bedroom. Ralph had fallen over. He was a big man – maybe 270 pounds. She couldn't turn him over. She panicked and ran out of the house, running down two flights of stairs, screaming and yelling for help. The police had come. Then she called my husband. Who in turn, called our son Anthony to meet him at Mary and Ralph's apartment on Court Street.

It was very sad. Especially for Nick. While Ralph Sr. was his stepfather, he was good to Nick. He treated him like his own son. He had been married to Mary for over forty-five years. They were married when he came back from the South Pacific after his tour of duty in the Navy where he served on the USS Hornet until 1947.

Unfortunately, for Nick, he and his father, they had had an argument a few days before his death. Something stupid. It was always something stupid. During this time, the girl he was dating had become pregnant, and Grandpa Ralph would never get to see Nick's only child. The second granddaughter Ralph would have fussed over.

Nick grieved. We all did. Big Ralph's demeanor was that of a tough guy. But he was really a Teddy Bear. Mary was devastated. I couldn't look at her. I had just gone through this several years earlier with my own mother. I'd like to think that women from that generation – the Greatest Generation – were tough. But they weren't.

Around the time of my father-in-law's death, a singing group, Mike and Mechanics came out with a song called *In the Living Years.* If you look up the words and listen to the music, it was apropos for the situation we all were in.

It goes something like this: *I didn't see my father the day he passed away. . .*

Words are a great lesson for all human beings. We only have the living years to make the best of ourselves and our lives, and our lives with one another. I don't want to get too preachy. But depression has taught me a great lesson about life.

I throw this out to those of you who want to take it: Life your life while you can. Because it goes by in a blink. Too cliché? Perhaps. But it's true. I wasted a lot of time being sick. I'm just adding that in here because it's in my heart and in my mind.

The funeral was a mess. Too many stories that weren't true floated around, that my father-in-law was in debt and left nothing to Mary to fall back on. It was too much to absorb at the time. A man was dead and people were talking about him. Small Italian communities are like that. Everyone knows everyone else's business.

Mary only wanted my husband by her side – Nick was no comfort to her – he never even slept with her when her husband died like he said he would – Mary came between us – things like that are bound to happen. My husband Ralph decided that we should move away from the neighborhood where we were born and make a new life for ourselves.

Nick held this decision against Ralph for a long, long, long time. But he cuddled up to Mary and we know he took advantage of her. We have four children of our own. We had to step away or we'd be wrapped up in the dirt.

We moved to New Jersey. To a small beach community. We made great friends. We met an Italian couple from Newark. When Brooklyn Italians meet Newark Italians, sparks fly. Kisses are placed on cheeks. Laughter begins. Love begins. Friendships happen. We were never so happy living in Ocean Grove, New Jersey.

Our neighbors were great. Our beach was two-hundred and fifty feet from my front door. People name their houses in Ocean Grove. Ours was named *Angel of the Sea*, that displayed a picture of a guardian angel walking two children over the bridge. We decorated the front and inside our home with angels of every color and description. We were blessed and we knew it. Plus, we never had to drive to the beach again.

The ocean outside my window rocked me to sleep. The chaos I had felt before was shifting and leaving my body. I knew I was healthy. I was happy. I was indeed blessed. But we worked hard. Very hard, sometimes twelve hours a day, especially when we were on trial. But some to the problems followed us.

Our new friend from Newark, Leonard, had this statement he made us think about. You can never run from your problems: you take them with you wherever you go. He was right. Nick visited us with yet a new wife from time to time. He was never the same. He hardly spoke.

Jeremy Ross had gotten out of jail four months earlier for good behavior. Nick wasn't worried about retaliation. Nick was a mad man, not in the mafia, but he became a member of the CIA. I don't know how. But I guess they hire crazy people. Because Nick is certifiable. He's not playing with a full deck of cards.

This new wife is not a trophy wife, like the rest were. She's plain. She compared Ralph and Nick the first time she met them. In her opinion, her husband was more handsome. I didn't want to pick a fight with her. I knew I could kick her ass. Maybe!

I pretend I'm a lady. You know, highly educated. Got my degree at 62 years old. Then went on to study creative writing and publishing. I shoot my mouth off when someone pisses me off. And this bitch, she pissed me off. I'm a nice person, but don't get me started.

Nick's kid was cute as a button. But you could see the new wife was jealous of her. It wasn't her child. She had four of her own.

Nick's family said his daughter looked like Kristin. I didn't think so. But they did have the same eyes. Blue, blue, blue. Like the sky. Like the Caribbean. She was a chunky kid like her father had been. I hoped she didn't have too much of his DNA. That drug problem is insane.

In the meantime, my husband was transferred to Newark District Court. It would be the first time in our court reporting careers that we didn't have to cross a bridge or go through a tunnel to get to work.

CHAPTER NINE

NICK AND BIG RALPH

Before Big Ralph passed, Jude wanted to go to military school, instead of a high school in New Jersey. Nick was Jude's godfather and he and Big Ralph weighed in on the subject. "Let him go," my father-in-law said, "It will be good for him." Nick charmed in and said, "I always thought Jude wanted to be a cop."

He does, "Ralph said," but he wants to go away to school."

Jude always wanted to be a mounted police officer like my brother-in-law Frank was. He was more enamored by the uniform than the job. But Jude liked horses. He probably would have made a great mounted cop.

Before Ralph passed, my husband had a good job in the district court. We were able to afford LaSalle Military Academy. Jude was away at school when Big Ralph died. We spent many days at the Academy watching Jude perform in the rifle club and the honor brigade. He was a good student, but he wasn't happy.

When he was on medical duty one evening, a young cadet tried to commit suicide. He was not allowed to tell anyone about this. That's what he thought. He thought he couldn't tell his parents. He kept it a secret from us, and he became depressed.

I guess depression runs in our family. We tried as hard as we could to keep Jude in school, but he wanted to come home. In his junior year, he came back home to where we lived In New Jersey. He stayed in his room most of the time and only came out for bathroom breaks and for dinners. He was not a happy camper. We had to get him into a high school: he went to Saint John Vianny in Colts Neck for half a year.

That summer, after Big Ralph, died Jude was moody. I knew we had to get him back to LaSalle for his senior year. We called Brother Luke, and the brother said, "I believe Jude has a vocation. He's trying to keep it to himself. Yes, he was very moody after his grandfather died. Yes, he didn't understand what was happening inside him. Perhaps, you should speak to a priest that you are familiar with and try to get this kid back into LaSalle.

We spoke to Father John. He was an older priest that Ralph and I drove from Asbury Park to the

Church while we were attending at Saint Thomas More.

Father John was an old-timer. He had problems himself as a young boy. "Get him to a psychiatrist." We did. The psychiatrist saw Jude and said, "Your son is a 14-year-old boy. His hormones are all over the place. Keep him in Saint John Vianny for now, and then get him back to LaSalle for his senior year."

When September rolled around, Jude was ready to go back to LaSalle Military Academy. He did it for his deceased grandfather. He wanted Big Ralph to be proud of him.

Back at school, he paid attention in all his classes, he became a star student. He won many honorary degrees; we knew Jude wanted to become a politician. James Florio, the governor of New Jersey, a second cousin, Jude had asked James to speak at his graduation because of his stand on abortion.

Jude graduated from LaSalle with high honors. We pulled up in a black limo to take Jude out to my brother's country club where we had a huge celebration for his graduation. All my cousins were there. Joe and Terry were still alive. Jude had a great time with Bart, a second cousin on my sister-in-law Terry's side. And they are still friends to this day. They have traveled to Europe together, and places where they could be alone to talk. Jude had my brother's ear, and Joe was a great person for Jude to have as a friend.

Love hurts sometimes. I know this to be true. I had great friends, one of them was my note-reader, when he died from AIDS, I was devastated. Daniel, Rich's partner, had a wonderful funeral mass for him.

Ralph and I attended this mass at Saint Katherine's church in Brooklyn. Daniel had this to say about his partner: "Rich was a tiny man, but he knew how to worm his way into people's hearts."

Jude and Bart went into the New York City Police Department Academy. I hated the decision that he made to become a cop. I'm speaking as a mother now. I didn't want my son to waste his time on the people of the City of New York. I thought my son's life was too precious to waste it on being a cop.

That's when body building entered Jude's life. For a while, he pumped iron and had a great time, going to the gym, but he lost track of his days at Seton Hall. He set himself up for failure. That's how I characterized it. He took 8 a. m. classes and left the house at 7:30 for a forty-five-minute drive. He was always late, missing at least twenty minutes of his first class.

This was a time in my life when I couldn't take the bullshit. I was starting to have my doubts about Jude, but he graduated from the Police Academy. And we had another man in blue in our family. As if it was enough with Nick on the narcotics squad or in the CIA, or NSRA, or something secret, Jude was now stationed in Lower Manhattan. Again, life goes around in circles. This is where my father's parents lived when they first came from Italy.

Our family goes from one blunder to another. Ralph and I got Mary a job in the bankruptcy court. Mary hated to work. Although she and big Ralph drove Uncle Lou's bus for handicapped children too. But other than that, she didn't like to work.

Mary was a fashion statement. She loved getting her hair done, colored and blown out, she did her nails too. She was quite the lady. I should have been so lucky. I had to work. When you have four children, you must get your ass out of bed and go to work.

Nevertheless, Mary started to work downstairs from us in the bankruptcy court. She was Judge Duberstein's docket clerk. Everyone loved Mary. She was very loveable. But then Nick started to call her again. Oh boy, here comes trouble.

When Nick gets into someone's head, he doesn't let go, and now he was going to involve Mary in a business venture. Water! Yep, he was buying into a water company. San Pellegrino.

Nick, who really wanted to be in law enforcement again, couldn't pass the psyche test – he had been too battered to make the grade – he had this long-range plan on getting into the CIA, NSRA, FBI – if there are capital letters in its name – Nick was there.

He moved in weird circles. Like Lester Chambers became his best friend. What Lester saw in Nick, I'll never know. Ralph hated that kind of music. We used to dance to the Famingo's *I only have eyes for you.* Our wedding song was *Color My World,* by Chicago.

Nick played music that shook the house down. The sound of the gongs – all that loud music drove Mary crazy. But he was her son, and she loved him and now he was separated from his wife with the kid, and he moved back in with Mary. Let him drive her crazy. We wanted no part of it.

Mary gave Nick all the money she had in the bank, Money that was supposed to be shared by three: Mary, Ralph, Jr. and Nick. Money that the D. A. 's office had collected when Big Ralph died. They had a slush fund, and they gave it all to Mary. She was supposed to divide it equally between the three of them.

Not in Nick's mind. He was a sonofabitch. He spent this money on Pellegrino water. They had a route. Mary would go on this route once a week with Nick. She took vacation days off from the bankruptcy court. We were all embarrassed. After all, we had gotten Mary the job.

My husband was the court reporter for Judge Duberstein, the chief judge of the bankruptcy court. The judge had a great sense of humor. When he called Ralph into the courtroom to take a case, he'd call over the interoffice phone, and say, "Ralph, get in here with your piano."

Everybody loved Duberstein. I learned how to speak Yiddish in his courtroom. I loved my days when I sat as a court reporter for him. Ralph and I switched sometimes. He took Judge Feller if there was a trail, and I worked with Duberstein.

Duberstein loved making fun of debtors. Not exactly making fun. But joking around with them. One morning he had a Chapter 7 petitioner that said he was a magician.

"Come up here, Mr. Smith. You say you're a magician. Is that right?

"Yes, sir."

"Where is it that you perform these magic tricks?"

"Your Honor, mostly at bowling alleys, or party rooms for children."

"And what kind of magic do you do, Mr. Smith?"

"I make things disappear and appear again, your Honor,"

"Oh, really, is that so."

"Yes, your Honor."

"Well, Mr. Smith, I'm going to ask you to step closer to the podium. I'd like to show you something."

"Mr. Smith, is that your signature on the petition in bankruptcy?"

"Yes, your Honor, that is my signature on the petition."

"Just step a bit closer. I don't think you can see what I'm about to do."

Mr. Smith stepped closer to the judge.

"Mr. Smith," – the judge picks up a pen from his desk. "Mr. Smith, are you watching?"

"Yes, your Honor, I'm watching."

"Are you sure?"

"Yes, your Honor." The judge takes his pen and waves it over Mr. Smith's petition in bankruptcy. "Mr. Smith, poof, all your debts are gone. Now, that's what I call magic. Get out of here Mr. Smith before I make you disappear."

"Yes, your Honor, I'm going. Thank, you, sir."

"Go on, Smith, get out of here."

With that, Mr. Smith picks up his briefcase and runs out of the courtroom. Leaving the who gallery in hysterics. Duberstein isn't finished yet.

"Okay, who's next. Let's see if we can make some more magic!"

CHAPTER TEN

SAN PELLEGRINO

Nick dragged Mary all over NYC, trying to get customers for his new business. There was one place at the top of the building where my friends the Kane Sisters used to sing. I think it was called the Rainbow Room in those days. And Nick had an argument with one of its owners. Nick always had a beef to pick with someone. Nick and Big Ralph liked to fight. But since Big Ralph was dead, Nick was on his own. Should he beat this guy up and spend the rest of his life in jail or should he just ignore him and go on his merry way, and not make a fool of Mary.

This new wife of Nick's, she had it in for me. I'm not a fighter. I'm a lover. I love people and I wasn't getting mixed up in their shit. I chose to ignore her, and I just didn't look at her when she walked into a room. We had other funerals in the family. It was said, but people die. This time Uncle Frankie died.

Just like Aunt Angie, Cousin Rosie, and Uncle Frankie; they were all bookies. Uncle Frankie was dating my mother-in-law Mary, and she was taking care of his kids, Angelia and Little Frankie.

Little Frankie, that's a family joke; he was six feet five inches tall. He folded a pizza like you'd fold a napkin and put the who pie in his mouth in one swoop.

I remember those days like they were yesterday. The amount of people outside the church when Uncle Frankie died would have amazed the Pope.

They lined the streets, especially Court Street. He was a hero, not a bookie in their eyes.

Now, Mary was alone again. What were Ralph and I going to do? We already had my mother and Aunt Jennie living with us.

Do you think Nick would do something? No, he left Mary alone at Nick to cheat on his other wife. He was going back between Number 2 and Number 3, trying to not spend all his money on these women.

One day, Paul McCartney came into town. He visited Nick in Manhattan, and then took a picture with his daughter. She was about four at the time, and she had no idea who Paul was. "Smile for the camera," her father said. She did and had a beautiful smile. Your father may be a scum bag, but his daughter was a cutie pie.

I'm not writing her name here. Why should a child be exposed because her father was an idiot.

Anyway, Aunt Angie, the 400 pounder – Uncle Jerry's wife, came to my house and sat on my kitchen chair and broke it. Maybe I should have said that. I'm being snotty, which is my nature. She bought Uncle Frankie a set of funeral flowers that you would put around the neck of a horse.

On the top of the horseshoe, it said *Ziggy*; which means *crazy man* in Italian.

Mary finally went to work on Monday morning, and she was greeted by a man who said he knew her from the Rainbow Room in Manhattan, where Nick was selling bottled water. Who was this man?

The man's name is Jose – Jose had worked with Mary in the bankruptcy court, and he wanted to take her out on a date. Frank had just passed, and Mary did want to insult Little Frankie and Angela, so she said no, she couldn't date him.

The story is so long, my fingers are killing me. I don't think I can report it anymore.

I just want to finish this paragraph by saying to you: this is a crazy family. Aren't you glad you don't belong to it?

CHAPTER ELEVEN

POLICE DEPARTMENT

Nick had an interview with his old captain of his narcotics precinct. He wanted to switch careers. He wanted to go to Quantico. His captain thought he was nuts.

"Why FBI?" Aren't you happy in this precinct? You have a gold medal. You can be sleeping and still get paid."

"I want to be a secret agent. You know, like the ones in the movies. Get me into Quantico. I'm insisting."

CHAPTER TWELVE

THE WAKEUP CALL

Nick didn't want to sleep and get paid. He wanted action. Action like the FBI, CIA, give me some more initials. That's what Nick wanted. One day, he wanted to wake up and be a star; like to have his name in the headlines of the paper. The scum bag Ros got out of prison and Nick wanted a reason to kill this man for what he had done to him.

Ralph tried to reason with him: "You have a child. She's four years old. Do you want to be a dead father and a hero, or do you want to grow her up."

His present wife didn't like his daughter. She disliked her so much, she sent her back to her mother in Manhattan, where they lived near the battery park. Nick visited them on occasion. He tried to be a good father to this growing child. But his mind was made up; he was going to kill Ross. But he wanted it to look like an accident.

My husband and I worked in court in Newark. It took me five and a half hours a day to travel from Ocean Grove into the City. I had my own problems. I started to have issues swallowing pills. I didn't know there was a muscle in your throat that gets bigger with age. I kept thinking there was a pill stuck in my throat. And I was getting anxious every time I was working in the courtroom.

Ralph made an appointment for me to see our gastroenterologist. Doctor Terrany ordered tests to find what exactly kept getting stuck in my throat. I had to have anesthesia, which is not something doctors like to do for eighty-year-old patients.

I had to be asleep when they did this procedure. I had to be brave. I had to do it. I wanted to know what the hell was in my throat,

If you don't know, I'm going to share some interesting information. Did you know we have sphincter muscles in our throats? Now I know we have three. I had been to the hospital nine times in my life to figure this out.

One of my hospital stays was on the psyche floor. When I went in to take a shower, some rude man opened the door and found me grabbing a towel to hide myself.

It's extremely scary being on a psyche floor. I have had to be on the psyche floor three times in my life. The depression was that debilitating.

Some of the medication I had a bad reaction to. Some of it, like Effexor, was an old medication, over twenty years old. Maybe it wasn't working the way it was supposed to. Or maybe I was just crazy. Either way, I had to take care of these problems.

Eventually, Doctor Green talked with my husband, and I was weaned off Effexor and given a prescription for Cymbalta.

My husband had already retired. He stayed home with me. Eventually, we had to move. Our disposable income was what we paid in taxes to live in Ocean Grove, on the beachfront. I loved that little town by the ocean, but we couldn't afford it anymore.

Ralph retired at seventy. He watched over me like a guardian angel. My friends never saw me again. I hid myself in my bedroom in my daughter's house. Amelia Hope, my beautiful granddaughter, whom I called my *chicken*. She wasn't afraid of me, but she wondered what was going on with her Mimi.

"Mimi is not herself," Ralph told her. "She's just having a hard time. One day when you are older, you will understand. Things like this happen to older people.

"But Pop," she asked my husband, "Why is Mimi losing her hair?"

"It's the medicine, Amelia. It just isn't good for her."

But I was doing bad things. I wasn't taking my medication. When Ralph would hand me my pills, I would stuff them inside the couch. I'd hide pills in my jewelry box. I was losing a grip on life. I was also giving everyone a hard time.

I had been staying up late at night after taking a sleep aid. I watched the worse programs ever. I had dreams about the devil. I hallucinated that I was being followed. I didn't want to see people. I was paranoid.

Looking back in retrospect, I didn't know what was happening to me. A combination of not taking my medication and not sleeping – then I started not eating – I believed I had anorexia and that I was dying.

The commercial: *A mind is a terrible thing to waste.* I was wasting my mind, my intelligence and my soul. I had gotten lost. Music didn't help. Painting didn't help. I refused every idea that either my daughter suggested, or that my sons suggested. We went to different kinds of psychological doctors. I had given up on Andrea B. She had been my therapist for over fifteen years. I had given up on Doctor Green, my psychiatrist for over fifteen years. They were both from CPC, a behavioral clinic that I had been going to when I had my first breakdown at school at Wilkes University in my second year.

I was a rational thinking human being. What had I done to myself? I mean, we are talking about it now. Ralph and me. We talked about how I hid the pills. What was I thinking? Did I want to die?

Some part of me kept thinking about my mother Millie how devastated she was when my father died. I thought about Mary, how devastated she was when Big Ralph died. My friends from Newark. Leonard was devastated when Arlene died. I didn't want to go through this. I didn't want to see my husband die. What would I do without him? He is the love of my life. It could happen! He could die. Then what?

I can't answer all these questions. I'm still seeking out what went wrong with me. A combination of losing the house, missing my friends, not being on the beach block where I had so many happy days. That house with all the angels outside on my porch, inside in my living room and bedrooms. My garden. The birdbath. My friends. Our outdoor parties. It was all gone. I felt like I had been left in a forest and I didn't know which way to get out.

I was trapped inside myself and I wasn't getting any better. I stayed in my room. I didn't read. I didn't shower. I didn't watch television. I just sat on the bed and stared into space.

The drugs weren't working when I was taking them. I had poisoned myself by not taking them. Then one day, I began to stutter, like I was having a seizure. That was it. Perhaps it was the ninth time I was admitted into a hospital. Like a street vagabond, I was put in the corridor. There weren't any rooms in the emergency room. I had a pill stuck in my throat. That was always my complaint: something is stuck in my throat. I felt it. And why were they telling me there was nothing there. They took ex-rays. They looked down at my throat with lights. I had procedures where I was put under for them to stick a light down my esophagus.

Yeah, I wanted to die. I didn't want to live like this. Who would? But it would take months, years, before I realized I did this to myself.

Ralph was losing his patience. He finally hired a friend to stay with me for an hour. One hour to get a cup of coffee by himself. I thought of it as despicable. But I refused to get in the car and go with him.

On the days he got me out of the house, we might be fifteen minutes from home, and I'd say, "I have to go back home." I begged him, "Take me home."

CHAPTER THIRTEEN

DOCTOR JEFFREY BEAL

I was crying on this freezing cold Monday morning. I had no idea why. I thought I was getting better, but the scale showed I had lost another ten pounds. I was a 204-pound woman, who now weighs 129 pounds. My doctor was scared I was killing myself, and he wasn't wrong.

I didn't want to live anymore. I have no idea why. I just didn't want to. I needed to be observed by other doctors. I needed them to tell me why I was stuttering, and why I can't drink water.

"Ralph, take her over to the emergency room."

"Will I see you there, Doctor Beal?"

"No, you won't," he said, which sent me into tears.

I sobbed so much. It reminded me of when I was a child and I'd cry for my brother or I'd cry for my sister, but there was no one there, just Aunt Jennie. She was always there for me. My heart hurt. Why was I such a lonely child?"

Ralph took me over to Jersey Shore Hospital, where we sat out in the waiting room. There were no beds in the hospital. I couldn't imagine what it was like during Covid. That was when this all started for me. I was afraid of everything. Afraid of getting sick. Afraid I'd die. Now I wanted to die, and I didn't know why.

Fear is a terrible thing. It robs and mind and it hurts the soul. I felt like I had been talking with the Devil and it scared me to death.

My kids came to see me almost every day while I lived with my daughter Kristin. It was Covid that did this to me. I was fine before Covid. We sat in the backyard, and I tried to explain to them what was wrong with me.

"Is the Devil real?" I asked.

Jude said, "Oh, Mom, that's a myth. They tried to keep the people in the olden days in line. That's just a myth. It's the God of tribulation. It's not the God of love. Jesus is the God of Love."

I believed him. I thought about it. Then I turned to Anthony who wanted to tell me something. He looked at me like I was crazy. They visited me in the hospital and at Kristin's house. It was summer and I wouldn't take a shower. I knew my bed smelled and I smelled too.

I asked Ralph to change my sheets. "Take a shower he said, and I'll change the sheets."

I went in and took a shower for the first time in several days. I slept a lot. I didn't read anymore. I didn't use my phone. I was a mess. Then we got a phone call from Jude, who told us to get to Florida, that they were giving out Covid shots to seniors.

I sucked in all the strength I could muster, and we drove to Florida. I didn't sleep a wink in our car. Usually, a car ride would lull me to sleep. Not this time. I was overanxious.

We knew it would take us three days. I tried eating food on this trip. We generally stopped at Cracker

Barrel. I ate a bit of a pancake. Everything that used to be my favorite, was not my favorite anymore.

I used to eat eggs and bacon and pancakes. Now, I was lucky I drank a cream soda. It was the only thing I seemed to like. Cream soda and vanilla ice cream. Or Root beer floats.

My stomach wouldn't accept food, so now they had to find a medication that I took before I ate. It was pink and looked like Pepto Bismol. It tasted horrible. But I took it so I could eat.

In Florida, we got our Covid shots. Pfizer. We were inoculated against Covid, but I still didn't want to live.

I remembered my mother and Mary; both were fifty-eight years old. I didn't want to be a widow. So, I would rather die?

That just didn't make sense.

I had a death wish because I didn't want to lose my husband. What was wrong with me?

This is what I told the intake doctor on the psyche floor. They kept me there for a long time. I tried to participate in the programs. I tried hard to work on myself. People there were strange.

There was a doctor who said I could take my pills in ice cream. I didn't like him. It's my belief he knew he was giving me the wrong medication. They used several different types of medication, some names I remember like Depakote. Some were good and some were bad.

Some doctors are horrendous. One of them gave me medication where my hair fell out, another gave me medication where I began to stutter.

I didn't like these doctors. They were all hypocrites. Instead of taking the hypocritic oath, not to harm a patient. They harmed me. They made me crazier than I was. My husband decided to stay in Florida for both our sakes. He bought a condo around December of 2021, right in the middle of Covid. People didn't wear masks in Florida like they had in the Northern states.

Ralph decided to book us on a cruise with friends. I fought him all the way to the cruise ship. He gave me no choice, which was probably smart on his behalf. He was sick of taking my shit. I was forced, but we went on a cruise that year with friends, and we never went back to New Jersey. We stayed and Florida, and we are still there today.

We live in a townhouse by the ocean, and we have a pool in our huge backyard. It's a nice place, South Palm Beach.

We live outside the building while my son lived on the fourth floor in a double bedroom apartment; he was how we were introduced to The Mayfair House.

Jude is a farrier. Although, he wanted to be a mounted cop. He still has his hands on horses. He has great clients, but I'm not allowed to tell you, their names.

Jude is secretive about his clients. He works very hard; half the year in New Jersey, the other half in Florida in Wellington.

One day, he said, "I'm going to go back to school. So, like his mother, Jude went back to school at 47 years old. First, he went to the Royal Academy in

London for his master's degree in special equine medicine.

Then he went to Edinburgh, Scotland, where he obtained a doctorate degree in Eugine nutrition. He's a brilliant boy. Why he ever wanted to become a cop, I'll never know.

Jude and Christina got married on October 7, 2017, a day after my birthday. They were both older, so there won't be any babies in their future.

Jude holds a patent for shoes. Horses' shoes. The kind that helps a horse achieve greatness. Christina wrote a book about T. Wayne Lukas, he's one of the best trainers of thoroughbred horse racing.

We are all together now as a family: Ralph and me, Kristin and Amelia, Jude and Christina, Anthony and Maria, and Joseph and Dana. Then there are the pets. Who could live without pets? Not us; that's for sure. We have Zeke, my daughter Kristin's blonde lab. Anthony has Phara, a hairless cat. She's not doing so well; she has seizures, just like her grandma thought she had several years earlier.

Ralph and I live about a mile away from the Orange Man at Mar-a-largo. I don't want to be political, but he's an idiot. If you haven't guessed by now, *Idiot* is my favorite word. I use it like a noun when I can't figure out what to call someone.

I'm only 50-some-odd pages in, and I want to tell you so much more about me, and about Ralph. We feed the homeless three days a week. It's our ministry. When I get back to Florida in three weeks, I'll become a Eucharistic minister, something I had done in New Jersey for many years.

My goal has always been for children without parents to have at least one parent. That's my goal: A Mother Teresa Foundation.

CHAPTER FOURTEEN

MOTHER TERESA FOUNDATION FOR HOMELESS CHILDREN

I've always believed children should have at least one parent. It's why I became an author. I want to earn enough money to support this foundation. I know people who have foundations for cancer research.

Oh, that's what I didn't tell you: my wonderful husband Ralph had cancer twice. He was diagnosed with Colon Cancer and had major surgery and had infusions of chemotherapy through a port in his chest.

I've always wondered whether it had anything to do with the situation at the World Trade Center. We worked in Newark at the time, and we were standing on the highway when the second tower went down.

Then a couple of years later, Ralph had prostate cancer and a radical surgery, one that cut into his man parts, and it wasn't nice what the doctor decided to do. Ralph will never forgive this doctor and to be quite honest, I don't forgive him either.

But we are both strong people. We take what's given to us. We know that God will Bless us; and we listen to tapes by Wayne Dyer, and Wayne says: remember before you go to sleep at night to say these affirmations: I am good; I am happy; I am a survivor; I am love; I am loved; I am blessed.

We are blessed with four children and four grandchildren. Not every one of them are happy. But

I think happiness is overrated. If you don't find happiness in this lifetime, you'll find it in the next.

That's why Ralph and I have gone back to church. Church has become the answer for us. We feed the homeless three days a week, on our way to Pompano Casino. We are gamblers. It's okay to be a gambler if you know what you're doing. We play the slots, but we know from experience that if both of us play, we are going to lose. So, just one of us plays while the other watches. We have this theory. It isn't a famous theory. It's just a matter of time before you're going to lose all your money.

I can't lose all my money because I have a goal, and my goal is to make children find a happy home. I'm going to need to hire lawyers and psychologists. I'm glad I've had experience with these types of people.

So, while this might not be the end of the story, look for Nick Alanzo in the year 2025. He will be in the courtroom with his stepbrother Ralph. He's a manic waiting for it to happen. He's a crazy man waiting to fly. He will be there by hook or by crook. He will be at the Twin Towers when they fall.

CHAPTER FIFTEEN

IN CONCLUSION

My friends will always be my friends no matter where I live, or where I may travel in the world. We are lovers, not fighters. We don't allow anyone to come in between us. We write together. We cry together. We have dinner together. Sometimes we even read the same books.

Carol MacAllister and Wendy Lynn Decker are my strengths. They have given me hope, when I didn't have any.

I'm going to attach a segment of something I wrote after Carol and I took the first semester at

Wilkes University, now called Maslow Creative Writing Program. We listened to a tape going up to school that first day of the first time we entered Wilks-Barre, Pennsylvania. It was 2008. Our car ride on that Friday morning from Ocean Grove, New Jersey, set in motion the next so many years of our lives. From 2008 to 2024, this is how we rolled.

By the time I finished sharing my idea about *The Mother Teresa Foundation*. Nick had spoken to Jude. Nick was Jude's godfather, and it was on a rare occasion that they would speak to each other. Nick had guided Jude on how to get into the Mounted division if NYOD Blue. Jude had always wanted to be a police officer. He believed that he wanted to help people.

My son must have been in shock when he found out that people did want his help. There were domestic quarrels, where police slugged one another, husband and wives. By the time he got on the scene, they were sorry and were kissing and making up.

I had always told Jude that the police department wasn't for him. That he should go back to college. For the first time in several years, he listened to his mother.

Jude did another 60 credits at Riverdale College in the Bronx and transferred to Iowa State University where he played football. On the day he finally suited up to play in the Big Eight, he was knocked down by a linebacker, injured his back, and had to come home for surgery. He had a pilonidal syst.

He felt frustrated. Like he hadn't accomplished anything in his first thirty years. We had to remind him every day what a good person he was. Maybe he had a calling. If he is anything like me, I'm going to guess he had a calling. But Jude ignited this calling and bough himself a horse.

He named his horse *Curious George Constanza*. When Jude went into the barn to feed George whinnied like a child. Jude was his father. His friend. His keeper. George loved Jude.

Jude taught George how to dance. Dressage! And they both won medals. When George got on in years. Jude donated him to a girl's school for the blind.

I will talk a little about the universe and how it plays its games. Like his mother Jude used to a late bloomer and went back to school in his late Forties

School isn't for everybody. But I'm not old fashioned like my father. I think both men and women should have a higher education.

All my children are great. We have our late bloomers and our early bloomers.

Kristin is an early bloomer. She graduated college in four years. I'm a late bloomer as you know. I crossed the stage at Rutgers and accepted my bachelor's diploma when I was sixty-two years old. It was a dark and rainy night. We were in the middle of Camdan, New Jersey. We needed to find a restaurant to take Jude and Kristin, and Nancy out to dinner. I remember eating lasagna that night. I don't think lasagna in a restaurant ever tasted that good. It was the joy of becoming a woman of letters. I knew this wasn't going to be my last rodeo. I knew I would go onto study my master's in creative writing. I knew it wasn't the end of school for me. And I was right!

Anthony and Joseph, school wasn't for them. But Anthony retired from the city as a master plumber at 57 years old.

Joseph went to Toyota school and became part of a car dealership on Long Island six days a week. If they don't fire him again, he will be with this company for two years.

My grandchildren are great. Lauren. And Madison both completed their bachelor's and master's degrees. Little Joe is a licensed electrician

Amelia Hope, she's just the Apple of our eye. She's going to be a senior in September 2025. She a peer counselor and loves working with autistic children

I started this saga in 1973. My fingers are killing me. I'm going to say good night and sweet dreams.

CHAPTER SIXTEEN

BACK TO THE BEGINNING

After it was all said and done, we all had to sit down and rest. It was time to think about the state of the world and how the universe speaks to us in many ways. If it wasn't for Nick taking my son into recognizing that he wanted to be a cop and recognizing his love for horses brought him to this place in his life where he is today, perhaps he would have never married Christina, a wonderful person that he had met ten years earlier at Gulf Stream Park in Florida. Christina was an announcer at the track. She was young beautiful and from Montreal Canada.

She was a Greek Goddess, a mature woman, Jude hadn't met many of those in his life. She understood my son, and saw the man that I had raised, who was intelligent and smart, but he hadn't given himself enough credit for who he was.

I started this book introducing our son to you. He was part of one of the biggest graduating classes at LaSalle Military Academy, graduating with high honors.

Jude might have screwed up his first years of college, but his thirst for education has grown over the years. He's a late bloomer, just like his mother.

Jude became a farrier under the tutelage of Shamas O'Brady, the Olympian Farrier, who is world renowned.

CHAPTER SEVENTEEN

IN CONCLUSION AGAIN

The first time I left my home to attend graduate school at Wilkes University's Creative Writing Programs was January of 2008. I had always been flanked by a kid or two going out the door, well, more like four children were always at my side or attached to my apron strings.

The day had finally come to put on my big girl pants, brave a smile, as my husband and kids waved from the front stoop. My kids shouted to my husband as I entered my friend Carol's car, "Where's mommy going?" I had never left home without them.

They had sad faces being left with their father. I'm not ashamed to admit it that I was afraid of the unknown, starting graduate school in my sixties.

My friend Carol drove us to Wilkes-Barre, Pennsylvania while butterflies flew around in my stomach. It was cold and a prediction of snow made the broadcast weather report for the weekend in the Pocono Mountains; we made the trip feel like I had entered a dream-like state, where snow might pile up and close the parkways and Carol and I would be stuck somewhere and never make our mandatory Friday night buffet.

When we then decided to listen to a tape that I had purchased earlier that week, written by Natalie Goldberg and Julia Cameron on the *Writer's Life*. Things like "early morning pages" a concept we had never heard before, writing in longhand when first waking in the morning sounded interesting, along with a lot of other writing ideas.

The trip took about two and a half hours on an overcast Friday morning that smelled like impending snow. Bleak, bleak, and bleaker!

Upon our arrival, we were greeted by a slew of administrative helpers, with packets of our schedule for each of one of us. We met several other students getting their information, and about six or seven of us packed our cars and followed each other to the Best Westin downtown in Wilkes-Barre.

Carol and I roomed together, giggled a lot, because we had to be the oldest students attending this new semester of creative writers looking for their next potential career.

The banquet started about 6:30 that evening and the tables were filled with first-year writing students, faculty and administrative students that would help us if we had any questions.

The dinner was lovely. We were interspersed with faculty, so we'd get to know each other and then a question went around the table: "When did you first know that you were a writer?"

Was I a writer? I didn't know. Students answered shyly – some didn't have an answer. I had always considered myself a court reporter, because that was my job. A writer – I had written a young adult novel over several years, working on it when I had time away from typing transcripts for attorneys from my court cases.

When my turn had come to answer this question: I meekly said, "When I walked in here earlier today to pick up my first-year packet. " It was the only truth I had at that time. I had left my comfortable home, my children and my husband in search of a writing career. I told myself to get used to the title, you didn't come all this way to ultimately get stuck in a snowstorm if you weren't going to take this idea of becoming a writer seriously.

From that moment on, I never looked back. Although, on the Saturday morning, after the 501 Class had ended, I did make my faculty tear up, telling them, I had never left my husband and children alone. I guess I'd have to get used to the idea for at least the next three years.

Sunday, we went to church. A beautiful church in downtown Wilkes-Barre. If I thought Ocean Grove was a Victorian Town, well this town was ancient. Wilkes=Barre is an old coal miner's town, with underground caves and lots of different-style homes. The campus sits on a large piece of property donated by several wealthy people. I became infatuated with all these writers, but I selected an African American Woman, Rashidah Ismaili to be my mentor.

Rashidah was a poet; she and Carol hit it off. Carol is a gifted poet, and we were like sisters from another mister. Carol taught me some poetry and I had my first piece published, about the Wisdom Bench on Main Street in Ocean Grove. A lot of people fall through the cracks. Once they were millionaires and now, they are homeless.

I think that's when I first discovered the person who I wanted to be. While I wanted to be a writer, and be a famous author one day, I wanted most of all to be a good person.

I learned how to use an Apple Mac. I had never used one of these computers before. I learned a lot of things at Wilkes, now called Maslov Creative Writing Low Residency programs, I learned to be respectful of others, and how to use the library to do research. I loved Wilkes, and people there loved me. I always had a smile on my face. I was in my element, writers, educated people, doctors, lawyers, even a judge was taking the courses.

I met Julia and George. George wasn't feeling well that first semester. And we discovered he had cancer. My husband also had cancer. I knew I would use cancer as an ailment for one of my characters, but which one? I hadn't made up my mind.

I was ready. I was ready for it all. Give me a pen, give me a moleskin, give me a computer. Leave me alone in a room, and I will write about my day away.

"Hello, Ernest," that's what my husband called me every morning when we woke up to go to work. "Good morning, Ralph, are you ready for this great day?"

"I know, I am." Then I'd go into the shower and get dressed in my Chico outfits. I always looked great. Time to go into the courtroom. Time for some more fun.

Bonnie Culver was the administrative dean. She had blond hair and a great smile. I liked Bonnie immediately. She called Carol and me her *Victorian Beach Ladies.*

Carol and I were comfortable in Gennett's Best Western. They had a bar in the center of the building where all the students met at night after class for a drink. I wasn't drinking in those days, so I had a diet coke.

Monday morning was our first class. We met Mike Lennon (Dr. J. Michael Lennon), Norman Mailer's official biographer. I loved Norman's writing. I had read the Gilmore story. *The Execution's Song*: that's what Mr. Mailer had won the Pulitzer Prize for writing that book. I made it my business to win two Norman Mailer Scholarships.

The first scholarship took place in Provincetown, Massachusetts. After the Gay Pride Parade, my husband and I had lobster roll, and discovered that Billy Jean King was Norman Mailer's neighbor.

The second scholarship took place in Salt Lake City, Utah, with Kaylie Jones. She is James Jones' daughter. The same as James Jones who wrote From Here to Eternity. I'm really hobnobbing now. James Jones!

John Bowers became my 510 professors. He knew Mario Puzzo. He wrote the Godfather. I'm in with the big names, now. But I'm just Patricia A. Florio, but don't you ever forget that name.

I wish you all a happy and healthy New Year...

END